BADGER'S PARTING GIFTS

Susan Varley

Translated by East Word

This edition published in 1997 by
Magi Publications
22 Manchester Street, London W1M 5PG

First published in Great Britain in 1984 by
Andersen Press, London
Printed and bound in Italy by
Grafiche AZ, Verona

ISBN 1 85430 525 5

獾爺爺忠誠、可靠，他總是喜歡幫助別人。可是，他太老了，他知道他不久會死的。

Badger was dependable, reliable, and always ready to lend a helping paw.
He was so old that he knew he must soon die.

貛爺爺並不怕死。他唯一的擔心是，他死了以後他的朋友們會怎樣的感覺。

貛爺爺已告訴他們，不久的一天他會走入‘長隧道’，他希望到那時大家不要太傷心。

一天，貛爺爺看到鼴鼠和青蛙在玩滑坡比賽，他很高興。他喜歡看到他的朋友們玩得開心。他最希望的一件事就是他能跟他們一起跑一跑。但是，他的腿太老了，跑不動了。

Badger wasn't afraid of death. His only worry was how his friends would feel when he was gone. Badger had told them that someday soon he would be going down the Long Tunnel, and he hoped they wouldn't be too sad when it happened.
One day, Badger watched Mole and Frog race down the hillside, enjoying the sight of his friends having a good time. He wished more than anything that he could run with them, but his old legs wouldn't let him.

他回到家時天已經晚了。他向月亮道了晚安，
關上了門簾，把寒冷的世界關在了外面。
他寫了一封信，吃了晚飯，然後坐到了靠近
爐火的安樂椅上。他輕輕地向前往後搖著椅子，
很快就睡熟了……。他做了一個奇怪而又美妙、
以前從來没做過的夢。

It was late when he arrived home. He wished the moon good night and closed the curtains on the cold world outside. He wrote a letter, had his supper and settled down in his rocking chair near the fire. He gently rocked himself to and fro, and soon was fast asleep, having a strange yet wonderful dream like none he had ever had before.

讓獾爺爺感到十分奇怪的是，他正跑在路上。在他的面前是一條很長的隧道。他再也用不著他的拐杖了，所以，他把它留在了地上。他快快地穿過了通道，直到他的四隻腳再也碰不著地面。他覺得自己正在往下掉；但卻一點也不疼。他感到很舒服，就好像他已經從自己的身體裡掉了出來似的。

Much to Badger's surprise, he was running. Ahead of him was a very long tunnel. He no longer needed his walking stick, so he left it on the floor. He moved swiftly through the long passageway, until his paws no longer touched the earth. He felt himself falling and tumbling, but nothing hurt. He felt free. It was as if he had fallen out of his body.

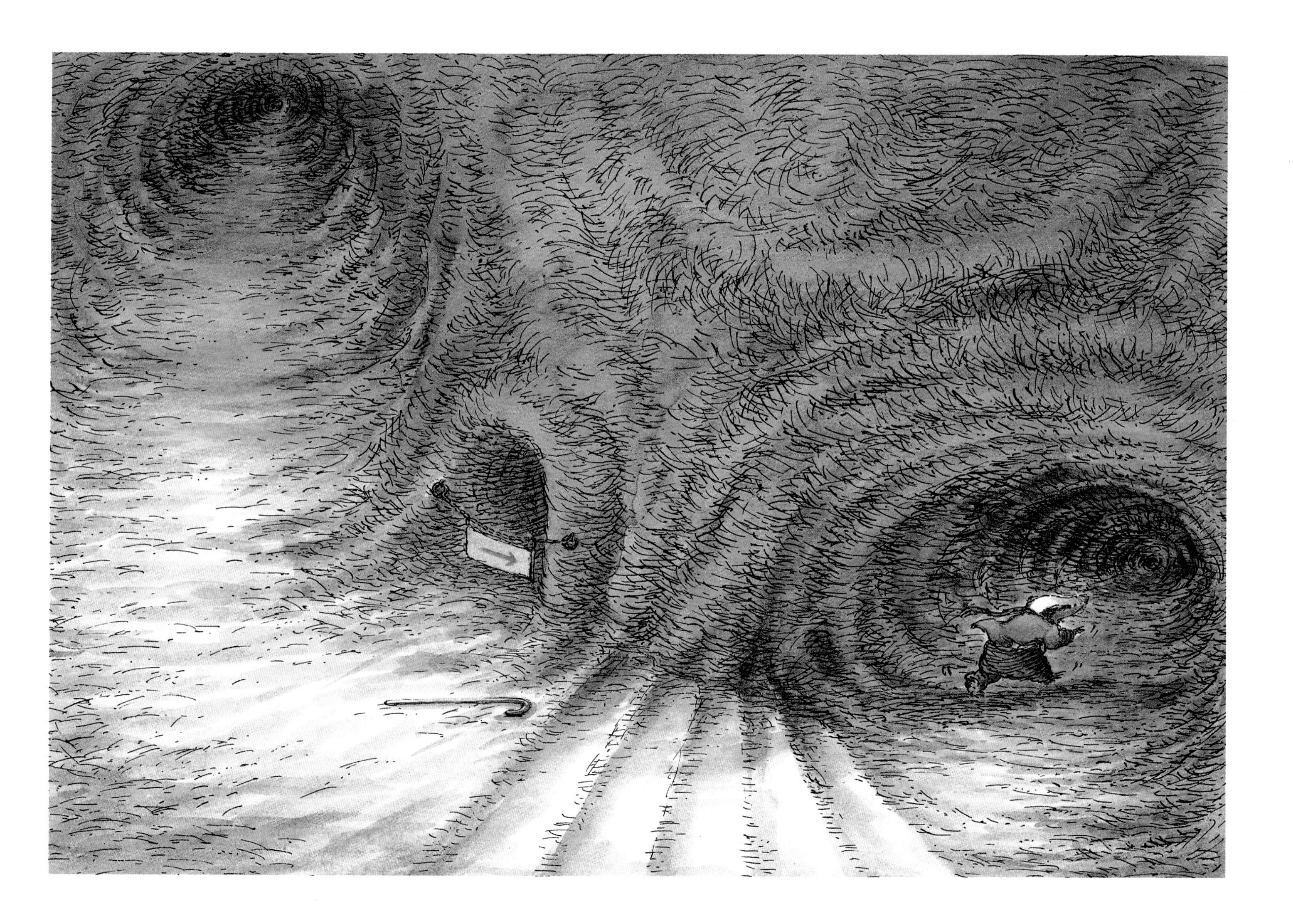

第二天，獾爺爺的朋友們焦急地聚集在他的門前。他没有像平時那樣出來向大家道早安。狐狸打破了謎團、向大家報告了獾爺爺已去世的消息，並念了獾爺爺留給大家的字條，上面寫道：“已經下了‘長隧道’。再見了，再見。獾爺爺。”所有的動物都十分愛獾爺爺，他們的心裡難過極了。鼴鼠特別感到失落、孤單，十分的傷心。

The following day Badger's friends gathered anxiously outside Badger's door. He hadn't come out to say good morning as he always did. Fox broke the news that Badger was dead and read Badger's note to them. It said simply, "Gone down the Long Tunnel. Bye Bye, Badger." All the animals had loved Badger, and everyone was very sad. Mole especially felt lost, alone and desperately unhappy.

BADGER

那天晚上，鼴鼠躺在床上眼淚不停地順著鼻子往下流，濕透了他抓在手裡用來安慰自己的毯子。在外面，冬天到了。

In bed that night Mole's tears rolled down his nose, soaking the blankets he clung to for comfort. Outside, winter had begun.

白雪覆蓋著鄉村的大地，但它卻藏不住獾爺爺朋友們傷心的情感。

獾爺爺在別人有困難的時候，總是喜歡幫忙。他告訴大家不要傷心，

可是要做到不傷心該有多難呀。

春天漸漸地來了，動物們又互相串門走動了，並談論獾爺爺活著時候的事兒。

The snow covered the countryside, but it didn't conceal the sadness that Badger's friends felt.
Badger had always been there when anyone needed him. He had told them not to be unhappy, but it was hard not to be.
As spring drew near, the animals visited each other and talked about the days when Badger was alive.

鼴鼠很會使用剪刀。他講到有一次獾爺爺是怎樣教他用一張疊起來的紙剪出了一串“紙鼴鼠”。他還記得當他成功地剪出了完整的一串“連腳紙鼴鼠”時，心裡那種高興的感覺。

Mole was good at using scissors. He told about the time Badger had taught him how to cut out a chain of paper moles from a piece of folded paper.
He remembered the joy he'd felt when he had finally succeeded in making a complete chain of moles with all the paws joined.

青蛙回想起獾爺爺是怎樣教他溜冰並在冰面上邁出了第一步。獾爺爺是那樣的有耐心帶著他練習，一直到他信心十足的自己溜去爲止。

Frog recalled how Badger had helped him to skate, and to take his first slippery steps on the ice. Badger had gently guided him until he had gained enough confidence to glide out on his own.

狐狸記得在他還是個‘小傢伙’的時候，他一直不會自己打領帶，多虧獾爺爺教會了他。
狐狸現在能打各種各樣的領帶花結，有些花結還是他自己編出來的。

Fox remembered how, when he was a young cub, he could never knot his tie properly, until Badger showed him how.
Fox could now tie every knot ever invented and some he'd made up himself. And of course his own neck tie was always perfectly knotted.

獾爺爺曾教給兔子太太怎樣烤制兔子形美味麵麭。她現在是位很好的廚師。當她講到她跟著獾爺爺上第一堂課時，她說她幾乎能聞到剛出爐的美味麵麭的味道。

大家都記得獾爺爺教的東西而且做得很好。獾爺爺去世前送了一輩子可受用的禮物給他們，以便他們可互相幫助。

Badger had shown Mrs Rabbit how to bake gingerbread rabbits. She was now an excellent cook. As she talked about her first cooking lesson with Badger, she could almost smell the gingerbread, fresh from the oven. Each animal remembered something Badger had taught them that they could now do well. He had given them a parting gift to treasure always, so that they could help each other.

雪融化之後，大家也不再傷心了。每次提起獾爺爺的時候，總是有人回想起使他們微笑的故事。

一天，鼹鼠在他最後一次看到獾爺爺的山坡上散步，他想感謝獾爺爺給他的去世禮物。他輕輕的說：“獾爺爺，謝謝您。”他相信獾爺爺會聽到他的説話。

很奇怪……獾爺爺真的聽到了。

As the snow melted, so did the animals' sadness. Whenever Badger's name was mentioned, someone remembered another story that made them all smile.

One day as Mole was walking on the hillside where he'd last seen Badger, he wanted to thank his friend for his parting gift.

"Thank you, Badger," he said softly, believing that Badger would hear him.

And . . . somehow . . . Badger did.